TEENS IN JAPAN

JAPAN

Teens in

by Sandy Donovan

Content Adviser: Guven Witteveen, Ph.D.,
Outreach Coordinator, Center for Japanese Studies,
University of Michigan

Reading Adviser: Katie Van Sluys, Ph.D.,
Department of Teacher Education,
DePaul University

Compass Point Books ✦ Minneapolis, Minnesota

Compass Point Books
3109 West 50th Street, #115
Minneapolis, MN 55410

Editor: Shelly Lyons
Designers: The Design Lab and Jaime Martens
Page Photo Researcher: The Design Lab
Cartographer: XNR Productions, Inc.
Library Consultant: Kathleen Baxter

Art Director: Jaime Martens
Creative Director: Keith Griffin
Editorial Director: Carol Jones
Managing Editor: Catherine Neitge

Library of Congress Cataloging-in-Publication Data
Donovan, Sandra, 1967-
    Teens in Japan / by Sandy Donovan.
      p. cm.—(Global connections)
    Includes bibliographical references and index.
    ISBN-13: 978-0-7565-2444-9 (library binding)
    ISBN-10: 0-7565-2444-X (library binding)
    ISBN-13: 978-0-7565-3193-5 (paperback)
    ISBN-10: 0-7565-3193-4 (paperback)
    1. Teenagers—Japan—Social conditions—Juvenile literature.
    2. Teenagers—Japan—Social life and customs—Juvenile literature.
    3. Japan—Social conditions—21st century—Juvenile literature.
    4. Japan—Social life and customs—21st century—Juvenile literature.
    I. Title.
    HQ799.J3D66 2007
    305.2350952—dc22   2006027057

Visit Compass Point Books on the Internet at www.compasspointbooks.com
or e-mail your request to custserv@compasspointbooks.com.

Table of Contents

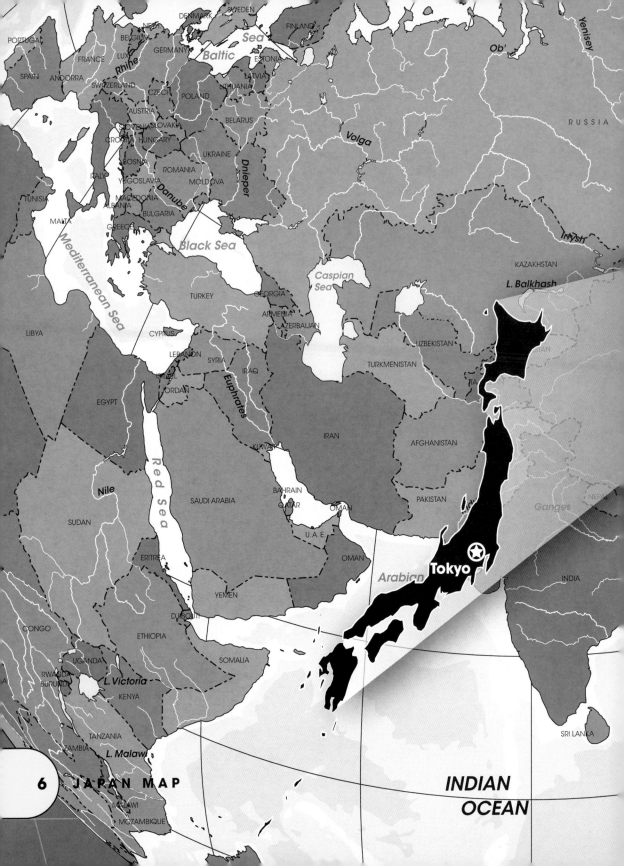

PACIFIC OCEAN

Amur

Lena

gara

L. Baykal

MONGOLIA

Sea of Japan

JAPAN

NORTH KOREA

SOUTH KOREA

Huang

Yellow Sea

East China Sea

CHINA

Yangtze

BHUTAN

BANGLADESH

MYANMAR

Salween

LAOS

PHILIPPINES

South China Sea

Mekong

THAILAND

KAMPU

Bay of Bengal

MALAYSIA

SINGAPORE

INDONESIA

7

PULSATING RAP MUSIC AND FLASHING NEON LIGHTS FILL THE INSIDE OF THE VIDEO ARCADE IN DOWNTOWN TOKYO, JAPAN'S CAPITAL CITY. A teenager sporting a bright purple Mohawk and a black leather jacket drops two 100-yen coins (U.S.$1.69) into the slot on the front of a *Dance Dance Revolution* machine. He watches while a digital dancer begins moving on the screen. This teen and his friend will spend all afternoon copying the dance prompts on the neon floor in front of the machine, singing along in English.

This mix of elements is Japanese and it represents many essential parts of life in Japan today. Japanese teenagers are familiar with cutting-edge technology. Their fashion sense reflects a desire to be different from their parents' generation and to stand out in a crowd. But in fact, a deep respect for the crowd and for belonging to a group is at the heart of Japanese culture. Japan's culture encourages people to conform, to look and act like everyone else. Japanese people have passed down traditions for centuries and are extremely proud of being Japanese and unlike the rest of the world.

9

Because the birth rate in Japan is low, at just 9.37 births per 1,000 people in 2006, the number of primary and secondary institutions is declining.

CHAPTER ONE

Pressure to Succeed

THE CONGESTED STREETS OF TOKYO ARE BUSTLING AT 8 A.M. Buses, trucks, small cars, and bicycles jam the intersections. People cram the sidewalks, headed to work or school. It's easy to pick out the students because most of them wear uniforms such as navy blue jackets or sailor shirts. Often a designated "big brother" or "big sister" accompanies younger children. These students are not really family members. They have been paired with younger students to make sure everyone arrives safely.

All Japanese children are required to attend elementary and middle school. Elementary school begins at age 6 and lasts for six years. Middle school lasts for three years. Most elementary and middle schools are public and co-educational, teaching both boys and girls. At age 14, students have to pass a series of competitive exams to be accepted into high school. Although attending high school is optional, more than 95 percent of Japanese teenagers go on to high school—either vocational, commercial, college preparatory, or for farming and fishing.

School Days

A school day in Japan reflects the country's values of routine, tradition, and putting the group before the individual. Upon arriving at school, students take off their shoes and put on indoor shoes. Japanese people rarely wear shoes in homes, schools, temples, or restaurants. This custom of respect also helps to keep homes and public places clean. Once students are in their indoor shoes, the day begins with an all-school meeting called *chorei*. An older student reads

chorei
chohr-eye

Schools often have shelves on which students store their outdoor shoes.

Teen Scenes

In downtown Tokyo, a 15-year-old boy hops out of bed before 6 A.M. He stuffs books, pens, and notebooks into his backpack, and grabs a banana and his MP3 player. Taking the elevator down to the ground floor of his family's apartment building, the boy adjusts his headphones and thinks about the day in front of him. His journey to school takes more than an hour. He rides a bus and two subway trains to reach his elite high school. After seven hours of school, he'll receive private tutoring and study more. It's a lot of studying, but he knows he needs it to reach his goal: being accepted at the University of Tokyo, where his father went, and receiving a prestigious job offer after graduating. As the son of a wealthy businessman, he knows he has a good chance of getting into a university, but he needs excellent grades to get into a top school.

Outside Tokyo, in a small suburban town, another 15-year-old student also wakes up early. She folds up her futon and stows it in a shallow closet before laying out breakfast for herself and her parents: chilled eel and a bean-paste soup. She too has a busy day in front of her. She will work for two hours in her parents' small grocery store before heading to school. After school, she tries to fit in several hours of studying before she returns to the store to help close up for the day. She wishes she had time to hang out with her friends, but she knows her parents need her help and she does not want to let them down.

In a small fishing village on Japan's coast, another teen has been up since 3 A.M. With his father and grandfather, he has been fishing in the calm early-morning water. Today they have made a good catch, and the boy knows they will be able to head in early enough for him to make it to school by mid-morning. He tries hard to get to school as often as possible, hoping that he can get good enough grades to be accepted to a technical college or university. He would like to learn something other than fishing, although his family has been fishermen for hundreds of years.

announcements and may lead the class in a song. Many large Japanese companies begin the day the same way.

Inside the classroom, students sit at desks in neat rows. Elementary students stay in the same classroom, with the same teacher, all day long. Although the classrooms may look quite traditional, with desks lined up in rows, almost all Japanese schools have modern technologies such as computers and Internet access. In middle and high school, students may select different courses and change classrooms and teachers throughout the day. Students must focus heavily on memorizing and repeating what they learn. A typical high school class period consists of teachers delivering information to students, and there may be little conversation about issues.

Lunch at Japanese elementary schools is typically a group activity. The meal is cooked at school and often consists of fish, rice, and vegetables. It might also include potatoes, bread, or noodles. One or two students may be asked to be the lunch servers for their classrooms each week. These lunch helpers wear masks and plastic gloves to keep germs away from the food. They stand at a serving table and serve portions to their classmates, who carry their meals to their desks where they all eat together. In larger schools, food is delivered on a cart to each classroom, and the students bunch their desks together to form tables. Middle schools and high schools don't offer lunch, so students

either bring their own meal from home or visit a snack shop at lunchtime.

Students also are required to do chores at their schools. Elementary and middle school students are usually assigned to a team, and the team is assigned weekly chores such

Students at a school in Tokyo serve lunch to their classmates.

as cleaning the hallways or toilets, cleaning the classroom, or weeding and sweeping the school grounds. These tasks reinforce the value that the Japanese place on taking care of the community and the group.

Studying Hard

In elementary school, Japanese students study subjects such as reading, writing, social studies, arithmetic, science, life environmental studies, music, arts and crafts, physical education, and home-making. But learning to read and write

Japanese is much more involved than learning to read and write English. Students continue to study Japanese through all of high school.

There are two main styles of Japanese writing: One system, called *kanji*, uses characters borrowed from Chinese. These can be root words or whole words. By the time they graduate from high school Japanese teens have memorized almost 2,000 of these characters. The second system is called *kana*. In kana, characters represent syllables instead of whole words. Japanese writing mixes kana and kanji characters together, including occasional words written with the Roman alphabet, so students need to learn all three well.

All elementary and middle school students participate in extracurricular activities, a moral education course, and integrated study with the theme chosen by the teacher—who might focus on international understanding,

kanji
kahn-jee
kana
kah-nah

Middle school students in Karuizwa practice their brushwork in a calligraphy class.

Kanji

Kanji are complex Chinese characters that the Japanese long ago adapted to serve for writing. Unlike Chinese, in which each character has one reading, Japanese characters can have several readings: That is, each character can have one or more Chinese sounds and one or more Japanese sounds, depending on the phrase or word in which it appears. Because of this, it is sometimes difficult to know the correct pronunciation of the names of people or places.

There are literally thousands of kanji characters, some with very complex, detailed brushstrokes. Learning kanji characters is the most difficult task in Japanese schools, and it frustrates some students. The Japanese government has limited the number of kanji used in the Japanese language—currently there are 1,945 official kanji characters in Japanese. That's still a lot of detail for students to learn, and if they want to read much Japanese literature, they need to learn even more. Novelists use far more than 2,000 kanji characters to make their language as precise as they like it.

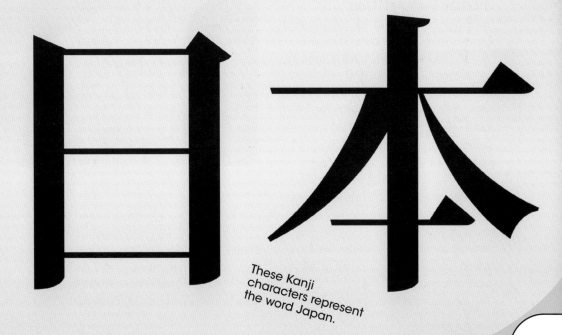

These Kanji characters represent the word Japan.

the environment, or volunteer activities such as cleaning up in the neighborhood. In middle school, students also begin to study a foreign language. Three-quarters of all students choose English as their foreign language, with the rest choosing to study other Asian or European languages.

Japanese citizens place a high value on the arts. All students learn to play a musical instrument in elementary school. They also learn traditional Japanese crafts such as watercolor painting, and origami, which is creating forms through paper folding. During their three years of high school, most students take 12 classes of arts, including music, fine art, crafts, and calligraphy.

Intense Competition

From their first years in school, Japanese students struggle and know they will have to work extremely hard to make it into a good high school and university. The competition is fierce and causes many children to worry and be stressed about school from a very young age. Students who do not do well may feel a great deal of shame about their performance. Students are not held back if they fail to learn a subject. All children move ahead to the next grade each year, but based on entrance exam cut-off scores, students are either kept in the lowest-ranked schools or are allowed to attend the best schools.

Japanese students spend a lot of

Wearing headbands written with the motto "Sure to pass the exam," 30 teens start a six-day program costing 576,000 yen (U.S.$4,875) to help them pass the entrance exam of an elite junior high school.

time on schoolwork—both in and out of school. School days are close to seven hours a day, Monday through Friday. But even in elementary school, Japanese students are expected to spend three or four hours per day on homework.

Students attend three semesters per year with up to one month off between each semester: April through July, September through December, and January through March.

During middle school, more than half of all students also attend the private after-school "cram schools" known as *juku*. At juku, students receive extra help to prepare for the difficult high school entrance exams. Juku are expensive and time-consuming, but the

juku
joo-koo

pressure to get into a good high school is intense. Admission is extremely competitive, and the fees are so high that only families earning above-average wages can afford to pay them. Only the best students can get into Japan's top high schools, and good grades are the way to ensure placement in these elite schools. All Japanese teenagers know that the way to become a successful business leader is to graduate from an elite university. And the only way to get into a good university is to go to a good high school. The importance that is placed on grades adds to the stress of being a teenager. In Japan, most people

A Typical Middle School Week

Monday	Tuesday	Wednesday	Thursday	Friday
Physical Education	Calligraphy	Physical Education	Physical Education	Physical Education
Social Studies	Japanese Literature	Social Studies	Japanese Literature	Social Studies
English	English	English	English	English
Math (Quadratic Equations)	Math (Quadratic Equations)	Math (Quadratic Equations)	Math (Quadratic Equations)	Math (Quadratic Equations)
Lunch	Lunch	Lunch	Lunch	Lunch
Biology	Biology	Biology	Biology	Biology
Scientific Experiments	Scientific Experiments	Scientific Experiments	Scientific Experiments	Scientific Experiments

According to the Programme for International Student Assessment, In 2003, Japan's 15-year-olds were ranked in the top class internationally in mathematics, science, and problem solving.

also feel that what you are doing at age 18 will determine how you will live the rest of your life. The result is a population of Japanese teenagers who feel intense pressure to do well.

One Japanese teenager explains the focus on college entrance exams at her high school:

"I am still in my second year of high school, so I have some time until the college entrance exams, but concern about the exams is never very far from my thoughts. Students at my high school take it easy during the first two years of high school, but about the time they enter third year, many suddenly change: They start attending juku classes and studying hard for entrance exams."

Most urban teens live in apartment buildings, while rural teens are likely to live in single-family homes.

2

Daily Routines

DAILY LIFE IN JAPAN IS A FASCINATING MIX OF MODERN CONVENIENCES AND TRADITIONAL CUSTOMS. For instance, a typical middle-income Japanese teenager probably owns many cutting-edge electronic gadgets, like cell phones, MP3 players, and video game units. But teenagers also spend quite a lot of time with older family members learning about Japanese traditions. This great respect for elders and for tradition is deeply ingrained in Japanese culture and is reflected in family living arrangements and daily activities.

For centuries, Japanese houses have reflected their owner's respect for order, nature, and simplicity. Traditional houses are made of wood and surrounded by elaborately landscaped gardens with neatly laid

A typical residential neighborhood south of Tokyo contains single-family houses with tile roofs.

out plants, cascading water or pools, and even bridges. Large sliding doors that lead to the landscape are often left open during the day to create a natural flow from indoors to outdoors. In the days before air conditioning, this helped to keep houses cool during the hot and humid summers. Today a traditional home with large gardens is still the ideal for some Japanese families. Very few people have a traditional Japanese house or garden of their own because of the high cost of land and the large populations of most cities. In city centers, most people live in apartment buildings. Because of the high risk of earthquakes in Japan, designers of high-rise buildings must submit a report demonstrating that their building will use earthquake-proof technology, such as super reinforced concrete frames and seismic wave-absorbing systems.

About three-quarters of all Japanese people live in cities rather than the country. But even small apartments in Japan's city centers are expensive. Land is less expensive outside of city centers, and many families live in suburban "pre-fab" homes that were made in factories and then put together on their lots. These houses have the simplicity of a traditional Japanese house, but instead of wood they are constructed of metal and synthetic materials similar to plastic. Rather than the large, landscaped gardens, they

are framed by neat yards covered with pebbles.

Inside a Japanese house, there is relatively little furniture, and most personal items are stored in large closets. At the front door, there is a spot for removing shoes before entering into the main living area. At least one room in a house is covered with floor mats called *tatami*. These mats are about 2 inches (5 centimeters) thick and are usually 6 feet (1.8 meters) long and 3 feet (90 cm) wide. It is common to measure the size of a house or a room by

tatami
tah-tah-mee

Recently, the average cost of an older 753-square-foot (68-square-meter) apartment was 35,607,000 yen (U.S.$301,396) to purchase or 450,000 yen (U.S.$3,809) a month to rent.

Futons are used for beds in Japan, but they are usually folded and stored in a closet during the day.

the number of tatami needed to cover the floor. A typical city apartment might have a kitchen/dining room, a bathroom, and two living rooms that measure about five tatami each.

During the day, the family watches television, reads, and does homework in the living rooms. At night, families use the living rooms for sleeping, and set up futons on the tatami. Japanese futons are different from the Western-style couches that fold into beds. Instead, Japanese

futons consist of a special mattress, comforter, and pillow. In the morning, the futons are folded and placed in closets for storage. Most homes have no beds, sofas, or chairs, except for in the kitchen and at children's study desks. People sit on cushions, rather than chairs. Many homes also have television sets, video game machines, and high-tech stereos.

There's one ancient Japanese tradition that many families try to keep

tokonoma

*toh-koh-
noh-mah*

today: having a *tokonoma*, or a hanging Buddhist picture scroll and a small, low table, which holds a vase of flowers and incense. Like many other Japanese traditions, the tokonoma sprung from a religious practice. Originally, tokonomas were private Buddhist altars where families honored relatives who had died. But over the years, they have come to represent the Japanese people's love of nature and beauty. Today, rather than a religious symbol, the tokonoma is commonly

considered a reminder of the importance of nature's beauty.

The Role of Religion

Most Japanese teenagers would say that they are not religious, and yet religion probably plays a greater role in their lives then they know. Because religion is so strongly embedded in almost all aspects of Japanese life, the Japanese do not always make distinctions between what is religious and what is secular, or not religious.

Most Japanese families follow two religions, Shinto and Buddhism.

Because both of these religions are

Although most Japanese citizens do not consider themselves to be religious, many people visit shrines or temples on important holidays or for occasions such as death anniversaries.

relatively flexible in their belief systems, it doesn't feel contradictory to follow both. For example, some births and weddings are celebrated at Shinto shrines. Shinto rituals are also used for launching ships and breaking ground on new building projects. A family may simply rent a hall for a funeral. But some funerals can involve the Buddhist practice of keeping the deceased body in a coffin with the head pointing north for 24 hours. After that, a Buddhist priest says special prayers, and the body is cremated. The family will wait until an appointed time to return to the crematorium to collect the ashes. Then the family will typically divide the ashes between a home altar, a parish temple burial ground, and sometimes the head temple of the particular branch of Buddhism they follow.

Shinto and Buddhism

Shinto

The Shinto religion is as old as Japan itself. Probably getting its start in the first millennium B.C., Shinto is based on respect and awe for nature and all life, as well as a love of simplicity and purity. The emphasis on nature and order can be seen throughout Japanese culture today. Even the way that Japanese food is arranged on a plate is a reflection of this love of order and nature's harmony. Several Japanese customs that grew out of Shinto remain today; for instance, taking off one's shoes before entering a public place stems from the Shinto emphasis on cleanliness and purity.

Buddhism

The ancient religion of Buddhism developed more than 2,500 years ago in India. There are tens of thousands of Buddhist believers around the world today, and many have slightly different interpretations of the teachings of the religion's founder, Siddhartha Gautama, also called the Buddha. But all Buddhists agree that people are reincarnated into new lives until they achieve a state of complete enlightenment, called Nirvana. In the sixth century A.D, Buddhism was introduced to Japan through China and Korea. Early Japanese Buddhists promoted acceptance of their religion by adapting some Shinto beliefs and building some of their temples on sacred Shinto ground. This slight melding of the two religions makes it easy for Japanese people today to follow both Shinto and Buddhism.

Starting the Day

Living in smaller spaces means that Japanese families need to be especially careful about keeping their homes clean and organized. Many teens don't have their own bedroom, so they lack storage space. In most homes, however, there are plenty of large closets, and throughout the day, items go in and out of them.

A typical day in Japan may start with the sound of a clock radio. But after getting dressed, Japanese teenagers will make sure their futons and other bedding are stowed in the closet before leaving for school. They may sit down for a breakfast of cereal and milk at a small kitchen table, or they may sit on a cushion called a *zabuton* for a more classic breakfast of bean paste soup, steamed rice, pickled vegetables, egg, or a slice of salted, grilled salmon.

For many Japanese students, going to school often means hopping on a bike, bus, or train. Because students are enrolled in schools based on their academic scores rather than the neighborhood where they live, a train ride to school may take up to an hour. In the country and in some suburbs, many teens ride their bikes to school all year long. In larger cities like Tokyo, students ride bikes or walk to a bus or train stop. Some who commute even ride on one of Japan's famous "bullet trains."

zabuton
zah-boo-tahn

A classic Japanese breakfast setting may contain fish, soup, and rice.

Bullet Trains

Shinkansen, or "bullet trains," have become a symbol of modern Japan. In 1959, construction began on the first line, which ran between Tokyo and Osaka. The sleek, white commuter trains were first introduced to carry the huge wave of tourists visiting Tokyo for the 1964 Olympic Games. The bullet-shaped trains can reach 186 miles (298 km) per hour, and they carry millions of passengers each day. During rush hours, the trains are so packed that white-gloved railroad guards are stationed on each platform to literally push commuters inside the closing train doors.

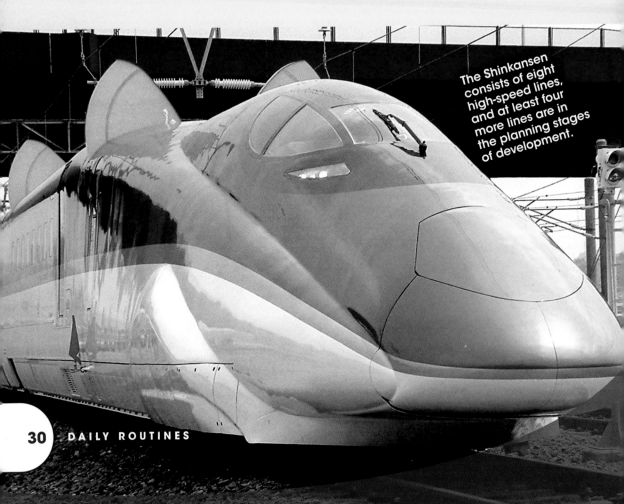

The Shinkansen consists of eight high-speed lines, and at least four more lines are in the planning stages of development.

The Art of Food

After school, a Japanese teenager may grab a quick bite at McDonald's or a corner convenience store before heading to music lessons or cram school.

In the evening, most teenagers sit down for a meal with their family—and this meal is vastly different from McDonald's. Although some families have higher tables and chairs, most families sit around a low table on zabutons. Teenagers who are invited to dine with other families know that how they behave during a meal is as important as what they say or eat.

Food is presented artistically in a way that represents both the variety and harmony of nature. Traditional Japanese staples include noodles or rice, seafood, fresh vegetables such as mushrooms and peppers, and soybean products such as tofu. Small bowls

Seafood and rice are combined with other ingredients to make sushi, a popular Japanese dish.

A casual restaurant in Osaka has zabutons on which customers sit and low tables on which they eat.

of each item are often placed on the table, and diners use chopsticks to serve and to eat. Nature's harmony is reflected in presenting small bits of seasonal or local food together, such as fish, vegetables, and rice. Color and texture as well as flavor are considered when planning a menu.

Boiled white rice is usually on the table for at least one meal, sometimes more. A traditional breakfast includes pickled vegetables and bean paste soup. Lunch may consist of salted fish and vegetables, and dinner often includes raw seafood or quickly fried meat. Japanese cooking styles developed in response to the country's temperature and geography. Plenty of seafood and fish have always been available along the coastlines of the island, but infrequently in the interior until the 20th century. Pickling or salting food was the best way to preserve fresh fish and vegetables through the long Japanese winters.

The Japanese have maintained many food customs throughout the centuries, including cooking style,

American Fast Food In Japan

In any Japanese city, you're likely to find international fast-food restaurants—McDonald's, Kentucky Fried Chicken, and Pizza Hut. The menu at these restaurants might differ from the menus of the same restaurants in other countries, but the portions are almost always smaller. For instance, a medium drink at a Japanese McDonald's contains the same amount of liquid as a small drink at a U.S. McDonald's. A medium pizza at Pizza Hut is the same size as a small pizza at a U.S. Pizza Hut.

But even with the smaller servings, fast food seems to be a bad influence on Japanese health. Several studies have shown that the recent popularity of fast food has brought about a jump in obesity and heart disease among the Japanese—two health concerns that the traditional healthful Japanese diet had minimized.

McDonald's restaurants in Japan have featured such menu items as the Teriyaki McBurger and a shrimp burger.

ingredients, and table manners. But as the Japanese lifestyle, particularly in cities, grows more harried, more Japanese are grabbing fast food. Some fast food is quite Japanese, such as sushi or rice balls made of sticky rice and pieces of meat, vegetables, fish, or pickled plums. But more fast food is appearing in Japan, including hamburgers, fried chicken, and french fries. One result of the growing popularity of these foods is that for the first time in their history, many Japanese are struggling with food-related health problems. Traditional Japanese foods such as fish and vegetables are much healthier for humans than hamburgers and french fries.

Wax models of sushi are displayed in the window of a sushi restaurant in the Shinjuku district of Tokyo.

Japanese Tea Ceremony

Although dining on fast food is becoming more and more common in Japan, one traditional custom remains popular throughout the country. The Japanese tea ceremony is a centuries-old ritual that focuses on respect, beauty, and simplicity. Originally the tea ceremony was for monks, samurai, and other elite Japanese citizens. Young girls today still learn the art of preparing powdered tea for guests. The ceremony involves special tea bowls, some ornate, but most very rustic looking. The presenter, usually a female, learns the correct way to mix the powder and to present the tea to guests. As with many Japanese customs, the presentation and arrangement are at the heart of the tea ceremony.

A formal full-length tea ceremony usually consists of a meal and two servings of green tea. It can last up to four hours.

Japanes teens are busy with their studies, so when they find time to hang out with friends, they make the most of it.

3

Social Groups

A TYPICAL JAPANESE FAMILY INCLUDES PARENTS AND ONE CHILD (the statistical average is 1.3 children). Japanese fathers usually work outside the home, while only about 50 percent of women have jobs outside the home. The role of Japanese fathers, however, is beginning to change. One Japanese father remarked, "It used to be that the father was strict and to be respected. But now, instead of being the master of the house, husband and wife are partners. It's a radical break with the past."

Traditionally, a father would leave for work before his children were awake in the morning and would not return until late in the evening, almost always after dinner and often after

A man and woman stroll with their baby in Shibuya station, in Tokyo. Many young Japanese men are proud of being "hands-on" fathers.

the children had gone to bed. After working at an office or factory all day, a Japanese father would spend a couple of hours at a bar or restaurant with his co-workers. They would have a drink, and perhaps take a turn at karaoke. Japanese companies encouraged this after-work socializing because it helped build loyalty among workers. For many years, Japanese men were worried that if they arrived home too early in the evening, neighbors and others would think they weren't dedicated or successful at their jobs. Today this idea is less common. Some businesses are shortening the work hours, and fathers are beginning to take on new family responsibilities. One Japanese father said, "Young men are saying they want to be much more involved in raising their kids and maybe the thing is they looked at their own

Women's Roles

Some Japanese fathers make arrangements to work from home, so they can take on a larger role in child care.

The norm in Japan is for men to hold down jobs outside the home while women take care of family and household duties. As with many traditional societies, men tend to be concerned with public roles, while women are responsible for taking care of children and elderly family members (including their own parents and their in-laws) as well as managing household budgets.

Today Japanese women tend to work when they are first married, leave their outside jobs once they have children, and return to their jobs once their children are grown. For instance, while almost 80 percent of Japanese women ages 20 to 24 were employed in the late 1990s, less than 60 percent of women ages 30 to 34 were employed. But it is becoming more common for women with young children to hold jobs outside the home: from 1994 to 2004, the percentage of working women ages 30 to 34 grew by 8 percent.

lives growing up, and not having a dad at home, an absentee dad, really was a burden for them."

About one-half of all Japanese women hold jobs, but many women leave their jobs at least temporarily when they have children. Even women who have continued to work full time have also traditionally been the main caregiver in most families. In the morning, they usually wake children up, prepare their lunches, and schedule their activities for the day. A Japanese family may also have grandparents living within their home, and women may take care of their own parents, their husband's parents, or sometimes both.

Traditionally, the Japanese value their elders and feel a big responsibility to care for older relatives. Until the 1960s, almost all Japanese teenagers had at least one grandparent living with them. High housing costs are another reason that extended families choose to live together. Today, however, it is becoming less common for extended family members to live together.

Submission Versus Independence

In traditional Japanese families, parents make all the rules. Teenagers are not encouraged to discuss issues or problems with their parents; instead, they are expected to do as they are told. Yoo Yoo Jin, a student at Senri International School in Osaka, explains how this tradition leads to clashes when teenagers are getting different messages from home and school:

"The school emphasized self-reliance and independence. But the culture of my family was dictatorial. My parents were always trying to tell me what to do, and even when I asked them to leave me alone, my mother would interfere. It was also part of our family tradition that you deferred to the opinions of your elders. At school, however, we were taught that you should assert your own opinions, and in fact, we did express our opinions regardless of the age of the person we were talking to. I do not think one should speak roughly to someone older than oneself, but when you don't agree with something, I think it is okay to say what you think. So that's what I did, even at home. My parents, however, did not seem willing to listen to what I had to say and would just insist that I do things as they had told me."

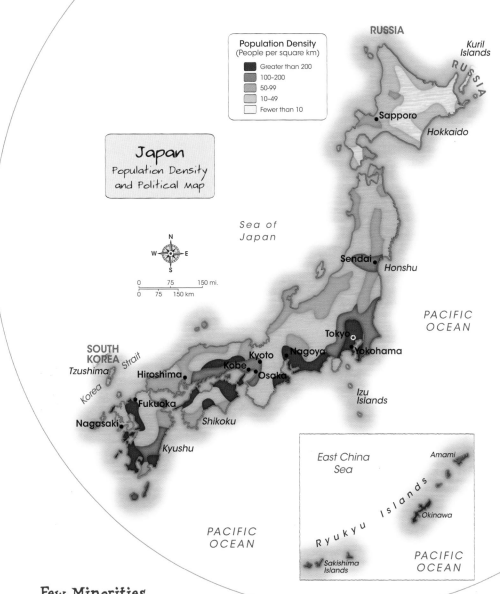

Population Density
(People per square km)

Greater than 200
100-200
50-99
10-49
Fewer than 10

Japan
Population Density
and Political Map

RUSSIA

Kuril
Islands

RUSSIA

Sapporo

Hokkaido

Sea of
Japan

N
W E
S

0   75   150 mi.
0   75   150 km

Sendai

Honshu

PACIFIC
OCEAN

Tokyo

SOUTH
KOREA   Strait
Tzushima

Korea

Hiroshima

Kobe   Kyoto   Nagoya   Yokohama

Osaka

Fukuoka

Nagasaki

Shikoku

Kyushu

Izu
Islands

East China
Sea

Amami

Ryukyu   Islands

Okinawa

Sakishima
Islands

PACIFIC
OCEAN

PACIFIC
OCEAN

Few Minorities

For most of Japan's history, the island country has not been invaded or taken over by foreigners. In fact, scientists believe that the people of Japan today probably look and speak much like the people who lived in Japan 2,000 years ago.

Looking around a classroom in a Japanese school, most of the students will appear quite similar. Not only will they likely be wearing similar clothes (maybe even uniforms), they will have similar facial features and similar coloring—usually brown eyes and straight brown or black hair. This is because most Japanese people today are the descendants of three streams of immigrants from Polynesia, East Asia, and the Altai region north of Mongolia. Until the 20th century, very few other people settled on the islands. Then large numbers of Koreans immigrated to Japan, during what is now called the Colonial Era. In recent years, foreign laborers and the grandchildren of some Japanese citizens who had moved to Brazil and Peru have moved to Japan.

There are some minority groups in Japan, and in the past they tended to live closely together. Today they are spread out. One of these groups is called Burakumin, meaning "hamlet dwellers." This group shares the same culture and ethnicity as most Japanese, but has been discriminated against throughout history. Despite Japanese laws declaring the equality of all citizens, other Japanese have looked down upon the Burakumin because they historically held "unclean" jobs such as butchering or leather working. Today about 1 percent or 2 percent of

There are about 120 ethnic Korean schools in Japan, including 30 high schools and a university.

all Japanese people are Burakumin, and although the government has worked to try to eliminate discrimination against them, many Burakumin still find it difficult to get jobs or housing in some parts of Japan.

Some large ethnic minorities in Japan are Chinese and Koreans. Many Koreans came to Japan, some voluntarily and some forced, to work as laborers in the country around the time of World War II. Today, about 650,000 of the children, grandchildren, and great-grandchildren of those workers live in Japan. Although some Koreans have been in Japan for four generations, it is still difficult for them to become citizens. They also face discrimination in housing, at jobs, socially, and even in schools.

Another small minority group in Japan is the Ainu, who lived on the islands and surrounding lands of northeast Asia long before historical

Girls attending a Korean school in Japan wear Hanbok gowns as their school uniform.

records began. Today there are only about 15,000 Ainu left in all of Japan, many of whom live in the Tokyo area. The origin of the Ainu language is unknown, but is unrelated to Japanese and today is rarely spoken. It is maintained by families passing down ancient stories and songs, myths, and rituals to their children.

Group Mentality

Glance around any public place in Japan and you will see people grouped together, either in families or in larger groups. Social groups of all kinds are important in Japan. Young people identify themselves by the schools they go to. As they grow older, they feel strong bonds with their colleges or universities, and, later, their jobs.

Teenagers in Japan make friends

Groups of pedestrians crowd a busy shopping district in Tokyo.

for the same reason that teenagers around the world do. Friendships are based on similarities and common interests. Because of the importance of groups, Japanese teens are more likely to hang out with several friends than with just one other person. With their busy schedules of school, extra lessons, tutoring, and sometimes working at part-time jobs or family businesses, many Japanese students do not have a lot of time for socializing. Often, they have an hour or so in the afternoons to gather with friends from school.

One custom that Japanese teen-agers often learn from their parents is gift giving. In Japan, gift giving is an essential part of most friendships. Small gifts are given for almost any occasion, and tradition often dictates what type of present is offered at what time. Just as important as the choice of gift is the presentation of the gift. Wrapping pres-ents is a complex task, and the choice of material—often intricately designed paper or silk—carries meaning, as does the method of folding and the choice of decoration.

Japanese begin to date in their teens. It is common for 14- and 15-year-olds to have boyfriends or girlfriends. But most couples get together for group dates rather than going out alone.

Friends' Names

Common Names

Japanese girls' names often end with ka, meaning "perfume" or "flower," or mi, meaning "beauty."

Male Names

Name	Pronunciation
Yuuki	(Yoo-kee)
Yuuto	(Yoo-toh)
Haruto	(Ha-roo-toh)
Souta	(Sow-tah)
Kouki	(Kow-kee)
Takumi	(Tah-koo-mee)
Kouta	(Kow-tah)
Ryouta	(Rye-ow-tah)
Haruki	(Hah-roo-kee)
Riku	(Rye-koo)

Female Names

Name	Pronunciation
Momoka	(Moh-moh-kah)
Haruka	(Hah-roo-kah)
Ayaka	(Eye-yah-kah)
Misaki	(Mee-sah-kee)
Sakura	(Sah-koor-ah)
Nanami	(Nah-nah-mee)
Yui	(Yoo-ee)
Hina	(Hee-nah)
Rin	(Rihn)
Honoka	(Hoh-noh-kah)

Women wearing traditional straw hats perform a dance dedicated to a wealthy crop, during a festival in Miyagi, in northeast Japan.

4

Festivals & Holidays

THE PARADE OF FOLK DANCERS WEARING SUMMER SILK *KIMONO* and flower-topped straw hats winds its way through the streets of the northeastern town of Sendai. It's the annual Tanabata festival, and the participants look almost identical to their ancestors who performed hundreds of years earlier on the same streets. Only the teenagers in the crowd watching—dressed in mini skirts and T-shirts bearing English slogans, cell phones pressed to their ears—mark this scene as 21st-century.

As the Japanese people strive to balance their nation's modern face with its proud history, festivals and holidays have remained an important part of life. Many of Japan's holidays honor the country's

kimono
kee-moh-noh

Japanese women participate in a festival at the Todai-ji Temple—one of the seven great temples located in the city of Nara, east of Tokyo.

ancient customs, and by encouraging people to dress in traditional costumes and retell old stories, they actively help people maintain ties to the past. Japanese festivals serve another important role: They allow people to relax and take a short break from the discipline and rigid standards of everyday life in their country. Businesses and schools close for several holidays each year, and on those days most Japanese dedicate themselves to celebration.

Japan's festivals often reflect the country's strong ties to the religions of Shinto and Buddhism. Some festivals honor Shinto gods, while others celebrate aspects of Buddhism. Almost all Japanese people, regardless of their religion, celebrate both types of festivals.

Christmas

Even though only about 1 percent of Japanese people are Christian, Christmas is becoming a popular holiday in Japan. In fact, Christmas Eve in Japan is a popular night for both romantic dates and parties with friends. Other large holidays in Japan include Ganjitsu, or New Year's Day, a weeklong spring celebration, and the summer holiday.

Ganjitsu

In Japan, Ganjitsu begins with a day of family celebration and honoring ancestors. Extended families usually gather together at this time, and families may travel a long way to be with each other; for many Japanese teenagers, New Year's Eve means an annual visit with cousins, grandparents, aunts, and uncles.

On December 31, most families

Young women dress in traditional kimono for a Ganjitsu celebration at Yakushiji temple—one of the seven great temples of Nara.

A mother and her son pray at Tokyo's Toyokawa Inari Shrine on Ganjitsu. Many Japanese visit Buddhist temples and Shinto shrines on Ganjitsu to pray for good luck in the coming year.

attend a Shinto shrine or Buddhist temple together. Some of the larger temples in cities like Tokyo receive millions of visitors that evening alone. Teenagers attend with their own families but often see their friends and classmates there. Sometimes up to a week before New Year's Eve, family members build a *kado matsu*, or a gate at their front door made of three bamboo and pine branches with a rope stretched through them. The gate is meant to invite in the spirits of friends and family, but to keep out evil spirits.

The next day, on Ganjitsu, or New Year's Day, families arrange a special

kado matsu
kah-doh maht-soo

National Holidays

If a date falls on a Sunday, the national holiday is the following Monday.

Ganjitsu *(New Year's Day)*	January 1
Seijin no Hi *(Coming-of-Age Day)*	The second Monday in January
Kenkoku Kinen no Hi *(National Foundation Day)*	February 11
Shumbun no Hi *(Vernal Equinox)*	March 20 or 21
Midori no Hi *(Greenery Day)*	April 29
Kempo Kinembi *(Constitution Memorial Day)*	May 3
Kokumin no Kyuujitsu *(National People's Day)*	May 4
Kodomo no Hi *(Children's Day)*	May 5
Umi no Hi *(Marine Day)*	July 20
Obon, or Bon Matsuri *(Summer Holiday)*	July or August
Keiro no Hi *(Respect-for-the-Aged Day)*	September 15
Shubun no Hi *(Autumnal Equinox Day)*	September 23 or 24
Taiiku no Hi *(Health/Sports Day)*	The second Monday in October
Bunka no Hi *(Culture Day)*	November 3
Kinro Kansha no Hi *(Labor Thanksgiving Day)*	November 23
Tenno Tanjobi *(Emperor's Birthday)*	December 23

table of traditional delicacies that have been prepared two or three days in advance. They include rice cakes, seaweed, dried sardines, oranges, and a whole lobster decorated with ferns. These items are not for eating; they are for decoration outdoors, and each element is meant to be a pun or wordplay. For example, fish eggs symbolize fertility and seaweed symbolizes longevity. The family eats a special meal of *zoni*, a soup made of rice cakes, vegetables, and chicken or fish. Adults exchange a traditional New Year's greeting at this meal, and afterward children receive presents called *otoshi dama*. Teenagers look forward to the gifts because they often receive money. Some make plans all year for how they will spend their otoshi dama.

zoni
zoh-nee

otoshi dama
oh-tah-shee dah-mah

Throughout Ganjitsu, people visit friends and family in their city or town. Each house prepares a stack of *jubako*, small boxes that are often used to hold leftover food. On New Year's Day, jubako are filled with small snacks for visitors. Relatives and close friends also bring otoshi dama for the children they visit. Although all businesses are closed for the day, there is a special mail delivery of Ganjitsu cards. Sending

jubako
joo-bah-koh

these cards to friends and relatives is a tradition, and the post offices specially mark these envelopes to be delivered on January 1.

Seijin no Hi

The second Monday of January is Seijin no Hi or coming-of-age day, a special holiday for people who will turn 20

Young women wearing traditional kimono participate in the annual Seijin no Hi ceremony at Toshimaen Park in Tokyo.

in the coming year. The age of 20 is the beginning of official adulthood in Japan, and the occasion is marked once a year by official ceremonies honoring those who have reached adulthood. Traditionally, 20-year-olds dress up, visit a shrine, and attend a ceremony with speeches by local leaders. However, in recent years, many older Japanese have been disappointed with what they say is a lack of respect by the new adults on this day. For instance, speeches are often interrupted by the ringing of cell phones, and sometimes the participants heckle the speakers. Some towns and cities have responded to this by trying to make the event more fun, and one town even moved its ceremony to Japan's Disneyland.

Golden Week

Over the past 20 years, April 29 through May 5 has become a weeklong celebration in Japan, with most schools and businesses closed during this time. Golden Week begins with Midori no Hi, or Greenery Day, a national holiday honoring Emperor Showa, or Hirohito (1901–1989). The beloved emperor loved nature and the environment, and so his holiday is called Greenery Day.

On May 3, Kempo Kinenbi, or Constitution Memorial Day, marks the day in 1947 when the new Japanese constitution went into effect.

Then on May 5, Kodomo no Hi, or Children's Day, is celebrated. On this day, families hang brightly colored fish-shaped paper or fabric kites from their roofs. Long ago, this day was

Giant carp kites are flown in Japan on Kodomo no Hi. Carp are a symbol of sons, and the kites are flown proudly from houses to indicate how many sons live there.

called Boy's Day, and many families today continue the tradition of wishing their boys good health and courage. A Girl's Day, or Hinamatsuri, is celebrated on March 3. On this day, families display collections of beautifully crafted dolls. The girls of the family then invite their friends over and serve them a special dessert while they all admire the doll collections.

Obon

The holiday of Obon, also called Bon Matsuri, is the largest summer holiday in Japan. It takes place in the middle of July in some regions of the country, and in the middle of August in others. Traditionally, it falls on the 13th to 15th day of the seventh month of the year—which is August according to the traditional Japanese lunar calendar, but July according to today's solar calendar.

During an Obon week ceremony, people place small, candle-lit paper lanterns on the river or sea as a memorial for the spirits of the dead. The lanterns are meant to help light the spirits' way back to the spirit world.

55

Japanese citizens dance at the Hayama Summer Festival, which is part of Obon. It is one of the few occasions when people dress in a lightweight kimono.

This Buddhist festival honoring the dead has become a sort of national holiday. According to the solar calendar, Obon is traditionally celebrated in the seventh month. However, according to the ancient lunar calendar based on moon cycles, the seventh month often coincides with August rather than July. Although Obon is more commonly celebrated July 13-15, many families take a special Obon holiday in August, making it the most popular—and expensive—time to take a summer vacation in Japan.

All Japanese people, whether they are Buddhist or not, celebrate this holiday by visiting the graves of relatives. They clean the graves and invite the ghosts of their relatives to follow them home for a visit. Some people hang colorful paper lanterns to symbolically mark the path to their house for the ghosts to follow. Some families decorate their homes with yellow paper lanterns to welcome the ghosts. It is quite common to see candles floating in rivers and lakes during this festival. It is believed that the luminaries guide the ancestors back to the spirit world.

During the festival, Japanese families act as though their relatives' spirits are visiting them. Special food and prayers are offered at meal times for the spirits. In many cities and towns, there are all-night festivals with music and dancing, sometimes featuring elaborate displays of fireworks. On July 15, families offer their "visitors" a farewell feast and then light a bonfire to help them see their way back to their graves.

Tanabata Festival

Although it's not a national holiday, Tanabata is an ancient festival based

Women dressed in costume and dramatic makeup attend a Tanabata festival.

A Japanese couple dressed in summer kimono admire the colorful decorations at a Tanabata festival.

on a Chinese legend about two stars falling in love and angering the gods. Tanabata takes place on July 7. In some areas, such as Sendai in northeast Japan, Tanabata has become an annual highlight that overshadows Obon. Several million people visit Sendai every year to view the city's beautifully decorated streets and take part in the Tanabata celebration.

Coming of Spring

Being lovers of nature, the Japanese have a special holiday to welcome the spring season. Setsubun—meaning literally "the splitting of the seasons"—takes place on February 3 or 4. People throw beans at someone wearing a mask representing a demon and chant, "Oni wa soto, fuku wa uchi," or "Out with the demons, in with good luck!"

During a Setsubun festival in Tokyo, children attend a bean-throwing ceremony, during which they toss beans at men in masks. The ceremony is meant to drive away evil spirits and bring good luck.

On a cell phone production line near Tokyo, cell phones are assembled by hand.

5 Working for a Living

DOING WELL IN SCHOOL IS THE TOP PRIORITY OF MOST YOUNG JAPANESE PEOPLE. The pressure to succeed is immense, and it comes from parents, teachers, and even friends. This is why the hours after school are often spent learning—either at music class, painting class, or a cram school, with little time left over for after-school jobs. But earning spending money is also important in this culture.

Although traditional Japanese culture honors simplicity and nature, the tech boom of the late 20th century turned the island nation into a hot spot for all things electronic. Japanese teenagers crave cell phones, Game Boys, and MP3 players every bit as much as Western teens do, but the fact that many of these products are produced in Japan

The fashion-forward clothing that many teens in Tokyo enjoy is often expensive.

makes them more common posessions of Japanese teenagers. Following fashion and other trends is important to Japanese young people. Because of this, Japanese fashion can get pretty wild. Although most Japanese people are born with dark brown or black hair, it's not uncommon to see gold, white, orange, red, purple, and green hair among teenagers hanging out in Tokyo or other urban areas. Some people say that the Japanese culture's traditional respect for conformity and routine has led Japanese teens to embrace just the opposite—leading to a particularly wild and colorful teenage fashion scene.

Harajuku

Some Japanese teens enjoy cosplay, or dressing up as anime, gothic, or Lolita (young girl) characters. It's common for teens who participate in cosplay to dress up and head to the Harajuku district of Tokyo. Sundays are often the busiest day for cosplay at Harajuku, and it is the best day for observers to see Japanese cosplay at its best.

In addition to cosplay, Harajuku is also known for its fashion boutiques and stores, such as the department store Laforet, popular for its trend-setting clothing for teens. The Ura-Hara, or backstreet Harajuku, is famous for its independent fashion boutiques.

This exciting mix of well-known high-fashion stores, small trendy boutiques, and cosplay, make Harajuku a true hot spot for teens.

For teens, having their own money to spend on activities such as cosplay is a way for them to be more independent.

63

Some teens work in retail stores to make extra money.

Of course, maintaining cutting-edge fashion styles can be expensive. Getting colorful streaks to stand out on jet-black hair is a long process and can cost as much as 11,820 yen (U.S.$100). A teenager in Japan can easily spend hundreds of dollars on imported clothes from Europe and America, and some visit tanning salons up to three times a week—for 2,364 yen (U.S.$20) a visit. Keeping up with the latest gadgets can cost plenty, too. Although much of the world's supply of electronic equipment is made in Japan, they are still expensive to purchase.

So, in between school, cram school, and extra lessons, Japanese teenagers try to find ways to earn

Cutting-Edge Technology

For decades, Japan has been a world leader in technological manufacturing. Japanese companies have been strategic about developing the most efficient, and therefore cheapest, methods for mass-producing electronic goods. In the 1980s, Japan was internationally known as an exporter of entertainment products such as televisions, stereos, and VCRs. Recently, it has become the world's foremost producer of communications and information-technology products like cellular phones, pagers, and electronic organizers.

Today robotics, or computer-controlled mechanical devices, is a hot field in Japan. Japanese factories have used robots for decades as a way of increasing efficiency. As a side result, many personal robotics products such as robotic pets can be seen throughout the country.

Shoppers look at the Aibo computer robot dogs at the Sony electronics store in the Ginza shopping district of Tokyo.

some spending money. Some Japanese teenagers have jobs after school or on weekends, often at fast-food restaurants. Others get allowances from their family for doing certain chores. Many Japanese teens may help clean up around their family's apartment, and those who live in houses may be put in charge of raking the a family's yard.

Teens in rural areas might help their families harvest rice or other crops and may not receive an allowance at all.

Despite the differences in ways teens earn money, many Japanese teens learn about earning and spending money at a young age, but they also learn to save money. Although Japan has banks, the post office is the most common place to open a savings account. Even children in Japan can deposit money at a post-office savings account and receive a small notebook, called a passbook, for keeping track of the account and making withdrawals.

Lifetime Jobs?

Since the end of World War II, large Japanese companies have basically guaranteed lifetime employment to employees. This feature of the Japanese workplace has been a cornerstone of the nation's culture of putting group membership before individual happiness. Large companies made it clear that they would take care of their workers, and in exchange, workers felt absolute loyalty to their jobs. This is the reason why Japanese men have historically worked such long hours, gone out with colleagues after work, and seen little of their families during the week. This loyalty to one job has been so strong in Japan that it is still customary for employees who are going home to bow and apologize to co-

workers who are still at work—even if it's 10 P.M. or later.

But in the last couple of decades, this rigid employment style has been weakening. With strong government

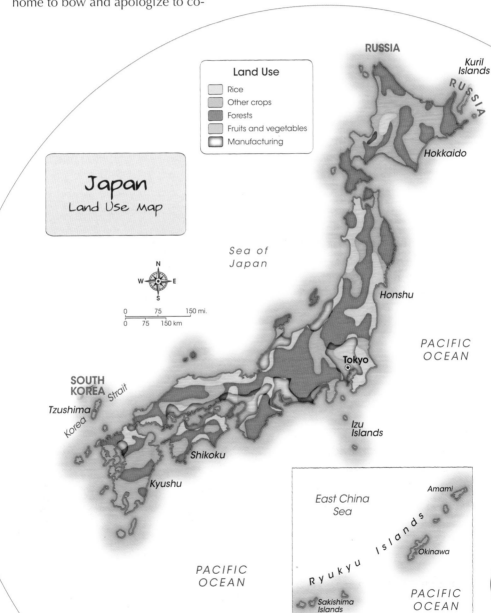

Japan
Land Use Map

Land Use
- Rice
- Other crops
- Forests
- Fruits and vegetables
- Manufacturing

RUSSIA

Kuril Islands

RUSSIA

Hokkaido

Sea of Japan

N
W E
S

0   75   150 mi.
0   75   150 km

Honshu

PACIFIC OCEAN

Tokyo

SOUTH KOREA

Tzushima

Korea Strait

Izu Islands

Shikoku

Kyushu

East China Sea

Amami

Ryukyu Islands

Okinawa

PACIFIC OCEAN

Sakishima Islands

PACIFIC OCEAN

Needed: Young People

With almost 130 million residents, Japan is one of the world's most densely populated countries. This means there are more people living per square foot in Japan than almost anywhere else.

But one thing there's not a lot of in Japan is young people. Japanese families are getting smaller. Twenty years ago, most Japanese families had two children, but today it is more common to have only one child per family. Less than 15 percent of the entire Japanese population is age 14 or younger. For teens, this means fewer classmates at school, and maybe even an easier time getting into universities and landing jobs than their parents had. But many people in Japan are worried about the decreasing number of young people. For one thing, with about 20 percent of the population older than age 65 and a longer-than-average life expectancy nationwide, Japan is going to need plenty of health care workers to take care of its elderly people in the coming years. Some Japanese are wondering how they will fill these and other jobs, and the government is considering options such as allowing more foreigners to enter the country or encouraging more women to take jobs outside the home.

Population by Age Group

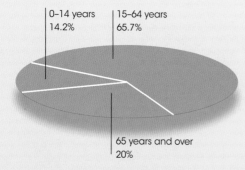

0–14 years
14.2%

15–64 years
65.7%

65 years and over
20%

Source: United States Central Intelligence Agency.

Labor force by occupation

| Agriculture | Industry | Services |
| 4.6% | 27.8% | 67.7% |

Source: United States Central Intelligence Agency.

support for manufacturing and other key industries, the Japanese economy grew at a rapid pace from the 1950s through the beginning of the 1990s. The country became one of the world's leading exporters of ships, electronic equipment, and automobiles, and a few long-standing corporations—which enjoyed complete loyalty from their workers—drove this success. But in the 1990s, the Japanese economy stumbled, and some foreign companies and executives were brought in to fix failing corporations. These foreigners brought with them many Western cutthroat business practices, such as large-scale downsizing, or firing of workers in lean times.

Today young Japanese workers feel less of a connection to their employers than their parents did, and it is more common for them to change jobs during their career. Many young people are more interested in working for a foreign company than a Japanese one, feeling that they are more likely to be rewarded for their own creativity and hard work at a foreign firm. They probably will still work the same long hours as employees at Japanese firms.

Seagaia Resort in the Miyazaki prefecture, on the south island of Kyushu, is the world's largest indoor water park. The roof opens during the warm weather of summer and closes during the cooler weather of winter.

6 Having Fun

OUTSIDE IT'S HOT AND HUMID, BUT INSIDE THIS GIANT DOMED BUILDING IN DOWNTOWN TOKYO, THE AIR IS CRISP AND COLD. A snowmaking machine blasts snow onto groomed ski trails and Japanese teens and adults swish past on downhill skis or snowboards. It's an indoor winter paradise. A few miles away is a similar giant arena, but this one is filled with sandy beaches and water. Waves are created from a machine and crash into the shore as families jump, swim, and lounge around on beach blankets.

Natural Playgrounds

Indoor playgrounds provide instant vacations for Japan's busy families, but are expensive. They are frequented by the country's wealthiest families. These families like the idea that, with the help of Japanese technology, they can instantly create whatever they need.

Most families in Japan schedule their vacations around the weather and travel to real beaches or mountains for outside sports. The climate of hot summers and cold, snowy winters provides a perfect backdrop for many outdoor sports such as hiking, bicycling, and skiing.

The many miles of shoreline

There are more than 850 bathing beaches throughout Japan.

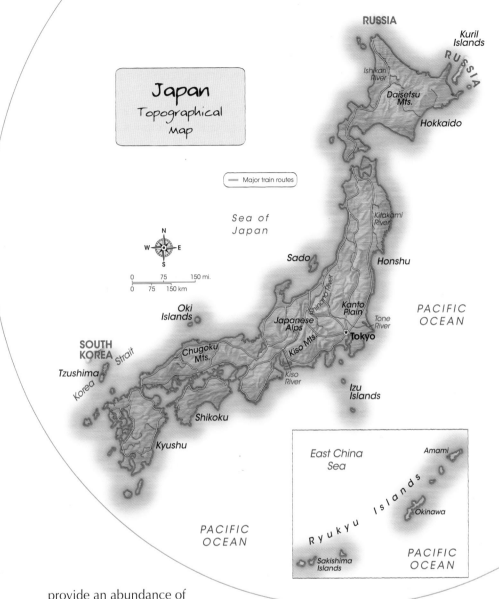

Japan
Topographical
Map

— Major train routes

RUSSIA

Kuril
Islands

RUSSIA

Ishkari
River

Daisetsu
Mts.

Hokkaido

Sea of
Japan

N
W-E
S

0   75   150 mi.
0   75   150 km

Kitakami
River

Sado

Honshu

Oki
Islands

Shinano River

Kanto
Plain

PACIFIC
OCEAN

Japanese
Alps

Kiso Mts.

Tone
River

★ Tokyo

SOUTH
KOREA

Strait

Chugoku
Mts.

Tzushima

Korea

Kiso
River

Izu
Islands

Shikoku

Kyushu

East China
Sea

Amami

Ryukyu Islands

Okinawa

PACIFIC
OCEAN

Sakishima
Islands

PACIFIC
OCEAN

provide an abundance of
seaside resorts. Most families
take vacations in July or August, and
many travel to the beach. With 4,000
islands, most of which are long and
narrow, there are plenty of beaches
to choose from. The country's largest
Island, Honshu, is only 230 miles

(368 km) across at its widest point, and
since most people live near the coasts,
they're never very far from a beach.

Japan is also mountainous, which
provides even more places for vacationing.

The Japanese Alps, famous for great skiing, are on central Honshu. In autumn, families may spend weekends hiking and camping in the mountains. During the winter, they go skiing or snowboarding at one of the many winter resorts.

National Pastimes

Many Japanese sports, such as skiing and swimming, reflect the people's love of nature, but other sports reflect the culture's respect for order and community. The Japanese national sport of sumo wrestling is a highly organized tournament sport that is full of rituals. Matches take place before audiences in round rings. The wrestlers often weigh more than 300 pounds (135 kilograms).

The Hakuba village near Nagano is a popular winter sports area. It features numerous resorts such as Happo-one, Iwatake, and Hakuba 47.

Mount Fuji Challenge

At 12,388 feet (3,778 meters) above sea level, Mount Fuji, or Fujiyama, is the highest point in Japan. It is one of several volcanoes in Japan, and although scientists classify it as "active," it last erupted in 1707. Centuries ago, Fujiyama was considered a holy spot fit only for priests to visit, but today it is a popular destination for world-class mountain climbers. During the official two-month climbing period each year, more than 200,000 climbers attempt to reach Fujiyama's summit. Several outposts dot the trail to the peak, where climbers can buy the water, food, and canned oxygen needed to make the climb. The summit offers an incomparable view of the sun rising over the Pacific Ocean.

Mount Fuji and Lake Ashi are famous tourist destinations.

Sumo wrestlers grapple with each other during a match at the Ryogoku Kokugikan, the grand sumo stadium in Tokyo.

The rituals of sumo wrestling are quite specific. Before each match, the wrestlers circle each other around the ring. They stomp their feet, clap their hands, and throw purifying salt into the air. All the while, they study how their opponent moves. When the referee, dressed in a traditional kimono, shouts to start the match, the wrestlers charge at each other. Their goal is to make their opponent touch the ground with any part of his body other than his feet or to leave the ring. There are 70 official sumo holds they can use during the match. Often it only takes a few seconds before one wrestler is down and the crowd cheers. Sumo wrestlers usually begin serious training at age 12 or 13, and they eat a

chanko
chahn-koh

special diet including *chanko*—a heavy stew of meat, vegetables, and eggs—to gain weight.

Sumo wrestling has been popular for centuries in Japan, but another spectator sport has gained popularity. Japan's second-most popular sport is usually thought of as being uniquely American: it's baseball. A U.S. teacher first introduced baseball to Japan in 1873, and it took off across the nation.

Its original appeal was probably the ritual and orderliness of the game, but recently the association with the United States helped to drive its popularity with young people.

Japanese major league baseball features the Central League and the Pacific League. Each league has six teams that play 130 games per season, ending in a Japan Series between the two league leaders. Today talent scouts often spend months in Japan, looking for hot new prospects to bring to U.S. teams.

Sumo wrestlers eat chanko, also called sumo stew, during the morning meal at the Musashigawa Beya sumo training facility in Okinawa.

Ichiro

Ichiro, the flashy, popular right fielder for the Seattle Mariners, is one of the few U.S. sports stars well-known enough to go by first name only. Ichiro Suzuki was a superstar in Japanese baseball in the 1990s before going to the United States in 2001 as the first Japanese-born position player for the Mariners (two Japanese pitchers had earlier signed with the team). That year, he was voted the American League's Most Valuable Player and the Rookie of the Year, becoming just the second player ever to win both awards in the same season. Ichiro lives in Kobe, Japan, with his wife, Yumiko, during the off-season.

Japanese people are as likely to play sports as they are to watch them. With more than 10,000 baseball and softball fields across the country, there are lots of opportunities for kids to play the game. Nearly every school has its own baseball team, and some of them borrow names from U.S. teams like the Giants or Tigers. Other popular sports are basketball, volleyball, tennis, and soccer. Almost all Japanese teenagers play some sport after school.

The martial arts of judo and karate have been popular in Japan for thousands of years and are now practiced around the world. Today these sports are often called self-defense sports, but developed as a form of combat and mental training among samurai warriors. They continue to be popular as a way of combining mind and body discipline. In a judo contest, opponents try to hold one another down, throw one another to the floor, or lift one another into the air. This competitive sport is now a feature of the Olympic Games. Karate is another form of fighting, but rather than throwing, it focuses on hitting and kicking. However, karate competitions today rarely involve bodily contact; instead, competitors are judged on the quality of their movements.

Indoor Fun

Japan is well-known for exporting cars and stereo equipment all over the world, but the Japanese are experts at another kind of technology as well:

The country is the home of much of the world's animated film. In Japan, cartoons are called anime (after the English word animated).

Storylines are usually fictional, although some may incorporate historical events. Anime spans many genres, including action, romance, comedy, science fiction, and drama. Anime is hugely popular with children, but there is also anime targeted at older viewers.

One influential, and still popular, anime film is *Akira*. Released in 1988, *Akira* is credited as one of the movies that brought anime back as a popular form of entertainment. At that time, most anime was cheaply done, recycling the same scenes where only the character's mouths moved. *Akira* was innovative, with detailed scenes, lip movement that matched the speech, and streamlined animation. Anime movies such as Hayao Miyazaki's *Spirited Away* and *Howl's Moving Castle* are becoming more popular worldwide. *Pokemon* and *Yu-Gi-Oh!* were popular in Japan before being exported to the United States.

A printed form of anime, called manga, is also hugely popular among young children and teenagers in Japan. Manga means "lighthearted pictures," but, like anime, spans many genres and interests. Manga authors write and illustrate the stories, which are first published in magazines like *Shonen Jump* and *Shojo Beat*. If they prove to be popular, they are re-released as a series of paperback books. Classic manga such

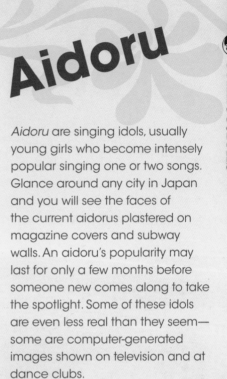

Aidoru

Aidoru are singing idols, usually young girls who become intensely popular singing one or two songs. Glance around any city in Japan and you will see the faces of the current aidorus plastered on magazine covers and subway walls. An aidoru's popularity may last for only a few months before someone new comes along to take the spotlight. Some of these idols are even less real than they seem—some are computer-generated images shown on television and at dance clubs.

Utada Hikaru is considered to be one of the most successful female pop stars in Japan. Her debut album, *First Love*, sold more than 8 million copies.

79

Osamu Tezuka

Japan's most famous manga artist was Osamu Tezuka, who died in 1989. He is often called the "father of manga" or the "Japanese Walt Disney," and is best known for *Phoenix*, a tale he began in 1954 and was still drawing when he died. Today, teenage manga fans flock to the Osamu Tezuka Manga Museum, opened in his hometown of Takarazuka in 1994.

The clock in Kyoto Station was designed by Osamu Tezuka.

Japanese schoolgirls shop in the Asakusa district of Tokyo.

as Osamu Tezuka's *Phoenix* and Akira Toriyama's *Dragon Ball* sell millions of copies each.

Hanging Out

When they do have free time, Japanese teenagers can be found hanging out with their friends, shopping, eating fast food, and listening to their MP3 players. Cell phones are also popular in Japan, and more than three-quarters of all Japanese teenagers have their own phone.

Most of all, Japanese teenagers enjoy seeing and being seen by their peers. A prime spot for hanging out is the Shibuya section of Tokyo. This trendy area is home to many dance clubs, record stores, video palaces, and karaoke houses. While Japanese music crazes usually imitate Western styles of punk rock and heavy metal, Japanese teens tend to follow fads with even more passion than teens in other countries. Some people say the popularity of brightly colored, punk rock hairstyles is an example of the Japanese teens' wish to stand against the conformity that makes up the culture of the country. Whatever the cause, it's true that Japanese teenagers take trend-following quite seriously.

Looking Ahead

FROM ANCIENT SHINTO TEMPLES TO ROBOTIC PETS, Japan is shaped by the contrast between its traditional values and modern inventiveness. The Shinto and Buddhist religions are at the heart of this country's ancient traditions. Cutting-edge technology and manufacturing reflect the nation's modern face. The traditional Japanese focus on conformity and the well-being of the group is shifting to reflect a new respect for individuality.

Young people in Japan today are living with one foot in Japan's ancient traditions and one foot in the modern world. They balance their culture's many ancient religious customs with today's modern conveniences. Most of all, Japan's young people are bridging the gap between the traditional Japanese society and a more worldly 21st century Japan. And yet, rebellious teenagers are still committed to the traditional Japanese expectations of working hard and excelling at school. These young people will help decide which pieces of modern life find a permanent home in the Japanese culture of the future.

At a Glance

Official name: Japan

Capital: Tokyo

People

Population: 127,463,611

Population by age group:
0–14 years: 14.2%
15–64 years: 65.7%
65 years and over: 20%

Life expectancy at birth: 81.25 years

Official Language: Japanese

Religions:
Observe both Shinto and Buddhism: 84%
Other: 16% (including Christian 0.7%)

Legal ages
Driver's license: 18
Military service: 18 (voluntary)
Voting: 20

Government

Type of government: Constitutional monarchy with a parliamentary government

Chief of state: Emperor

Head of government: Prime Minister, appointed by the Diet

Lawmaking body: Kokkaii, or bicameral Diet, consisting of the Sangi, or House of Councillors and the Shugi, or House of Representatives

Administrative divisions: 47 prefectures

Independence: 660 B.C.

National symbols: Fujiyama, rising sun (on flag), cherry blossom (appears on crest of Imperial Family), crane (indigenous to Japan, symbolizes peace)

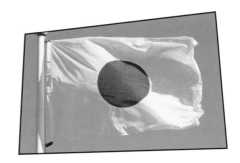

Geography

Total Area: 145,321 square miles (377,835 sq km)

Climate: Varies from tropical in south to cool temperate in north

Highest point: Mount Fuji 12,388 feet (3,778 m)

Lowest point: Hachiro-gata 13 feet (-4 m) below sea level

Major rivers: Tone, Ishikari, Shinano, Kitakami, Kiso

Major landforms: Chugoku Mountains, Kiso Mountains, Japanese Alps, Daisetsu Mountains; Kanto Plain

Economy

Currency: Yen

Major natural resources: Steel, gold, magnesium, silver

Major agricultural products: Rice, sugar beets, vegetables, fruit, pork, poultry, dairy products, eggs, fish

Major exports: Transport equipment, motor vehicles, semiconductors, electrical machinery, chemicals

Major imports: Machinery and equipment, fuels, foodstuffs, chemicals, textiles, raw materials

Historical Timeline

After many years of civil war, the country reunites; foundation of modern Japan is laid

Major earthquake hits Tokyo, killing more than 100,000 people

Japan is unified as powerful clan rulers emerge; Chinese written characters are introduced

 British colonies are established in North America

300 B.C.–300 A.D.	300–645	c. 1000	1568–1600	1600s	1895	1914–1918	1923

World War I

Inca civilization flourishes in South America

Rice cultivation, metalworking, and the potter's wheel are introduced from China and Korea

Japan becomes a world power through victories over China and Russia (1905) and the annexation of Korea (1910–1945)

Historical World Event

The People's
Republic of
China is born

The summer Olympic
Games take place in
Tokyo to be followed
by the 1972 winter
Olympic Games
in Sapporo
and the 1998
winter Games
in Nagano

U.S. military planes drop
an atomic bomb on the
city of Hiroshima on
August 6 and another
on Nagasaki on
August 9

| 1937–1945 | 1945 | 1947 | 1949 | 1950–1953 | 1961 | 1964 |

The parliamentary
system is established,
giving citizens the
right to vote

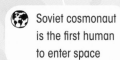 Soviet cosmonaut
is the first human
to enter space

Japan goes to war with China;
signs an agreement to be part
of the Axis powers during
World War II; Japan's attack
on Pearl Harbor, Hawaii, in
1941 brings the United
States into the war

 Korean War

Historical Timeline

Major earthquake rocks Japan, killing thousands of citizens; a religious cult attacks subway users in Tokyo with sarin gas

Japan and China fail to agree on who controls oil and gas reserves in the East China Sea

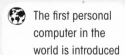 Terrorist attacks on the two World Trade Center Towers in New York City and on the Pentagon in Washington, D.C., leave thousands dead

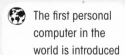 The first personal computer in the world is introduced

| 1972 | 1981 | 1989 | 1991 | 1995 | 2001 | 2004 | 2006 |

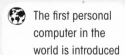 Soviet Union collapses

Japanese soldiers are deployed to Iraq for a noncombat presence; the troops are withdrawn in 2006

Japanese prime minister visits China and normal diplomatic relations resume

After Emperor Hirohito's death, his son Akihito succeeds him

Glossary

commute	travel back and forth regularly
conformity	action in accordance with some specified standard or authority
contradictory	asserting the opposite
devastation	ruins, chaos, or disorder caused by a violent action
discrimintaion	treating people unfairly because of their race, religion, sex, disability, sexuality, or age
distinictions	differences between
extracurricular	referring to activities that are usually connected with school but have no academic credits
ingrained	forming a part of the essence or being of a person or thing
martial arts	systems of fighting and self-defense, including judo, karate, archery, and fencing, that originated in Japan and Korea
Roman alphabet	the alphabet evolved by the ancient Romans which serves for writing most of the languages of western Europe
samurai	special class of warriors who fought for local lords in ancient Japan; the samurai code focuses on loyalty and obedience
secular	not specifically religious

Additional Resources

IN THE LIBRARY

Behnke, Allison. *Japan in Pictures*. Minneapolis: Lerner Publications, 2003.

Hartz, Paula. *Shinto*. New York: Facts on File, 1997.

Naff, Clay Farris. *Japan. History of Nations*. San Diego: Greenhaven Press, 2004.

Netzley, Patricia D. *Japan: Modern Nations of the World*. San Diego: Lucent Books, 2000.

Tames, Richard. *Hiroshima: The Shadow of the Bomb*. Chicago: Heinemann Library, 2006.

Winston, Diana. *Wide Awake: A Buddhist Guide For Teens*. New York: Perigree Book, 2003.

Woog, Adam. *A Samurai Warrior. Working Life*. San Diego: Lucent Books, 2005.

ON THE WEB

For more information on this topic, use FactHound.

1. Go to www.facthound.com
2. Type in this book ID: 075652444X
3. Click on the *Fetch It* button.

Look for more Global Connections books.

Teens in Australia
Teens in Brazil
Teens in China
Teens in France
Teens in India
Teens in Israel
Teens in Kenya

Teens in Mexico
Teens in Russia
Teens in Saudi Arabia
Teens in Spain
Teens in Venezuela
Teens in Vietnam

Source Notes

Page 21, line 9: Mizushima, Yu. *Deai: The Lives of Seven Japanese High School Students.*
www.tjf.or.jp/deai/contents/chart/mystory/myst_my_e.htm

Page 37, line 13: Sueda, Tomo. *The Changing Face of Fatherhood.*
CBS Sunday Morning. 18 June 2006. 20 Nov. 2006.
www.cbsnews.com/stories/2006/06/18/sunday/main1726667_page4.shtml

Page 38, column 2, line 8: Kingston, Jeff. *The Changing Face of Fatherhood.*
CBS Sunday Morning. 18 June 2006. 20 Nov. 2006.
www.cbsnews.com/stories/2006/06/18/sunday/main1726667_page4.shtml

Page 40, sidebar, column 1, line 11: Yoo Yoo, Jin. *Deai: The
Lives of Seven Japanese High School Students.* www.tjf.
or.jp/deai/contents/chart/mystory/myst_yy_e.htm

Pages 84–85, At a Glance: United States. Central Intelligence
Agency. *The World Factbook: Japan.* 2005. 20 June 2005. www.cia.
gov/cia/publications/factbook/geos/ja.html

Select Bibliography

Allinson, Gary D. *The Columbia Guide to Modern Japanese History.* New York: Columbia University Press, 1999.

CBS Sunday Morning. *The Changing Face of Fatherhood.* 18 June 2006. 20 Nov. 2006. www.cbsnews.com/stories/2006/06/18/sunday/main1726667_page4.shtml

CIA World Factbook Online. *Japan.* 14 Nov. 2006. 21 Nov. 2006. www.cia.gov/cia/publications/factbook/geos/rs.html

"Construction, Real Estate, and Housing." Ministry of Internal Affairs and Communications. 6 Oct. 2006. www.stat.go.jp/english/data/kakei/156bn.htm

Embassy of Japan in Washington, D.C., 20 Oct. 2006. www.us.emb-japan.go.jp/english/html/japanindc.htm

"Family income and Expenditure Survey." Ministry of Internal affairs and Communications. 19 Oct. 2006. www.stat.go.jp/english/data/kakei/156bn.htm

Globalis. *Japan.* 20 Nov. 2006. http://globalis.gvu.une.edu/country.cfm?country=JP

Kamachi, Noriko. *Culture and Customs of Japan.* Westport, Conn.: Greenwood Press, 1999.

Larimer, Tim. "From We to Me." *Time Asia*. 3 May 1999. 1 June 2006. www.time.com/time/asia/asia/magazine/1999/990503/home.html

McGray, Douglas. "Japan's Gross National Cool" *Foreign Policy*, No. 130 (May–June, 2002).

National Clearinghouse for U.S.-Japan Studies.17 Nov. 2006. www.indiana.edu/~japan/info.html

National Science Foundation: Science and Technology of Japan. 17 Nov. 2006. http://www.nsf.gov/statistics/nsf97324/chp1.htm

Osmond, Stephen. "Part of a Group: Conforming in Japan." *The World & I*. 12. 1 June 1997.

Shelley, Rex. *Cultures of the World: Japan*. New York: Marshall Cavendish, 2002.

Sugimoto, Yoshio. *An Introduction to Japanese Society*. New York: Cambridge University Press, 1997.

Index

About the Author
Sandy Donovan

Sandy Donovan has written many books for young people. She has lived and traveled in Europe, Asia, and the Middle East. She lives in Minneapolis, Minnesota, with her husband and two sons, Henry and Gus.

About the Content Adviser
Guven Witteveen, Ph.D.

Our content adviser for Teens in Japan, Guven Witteveen is an expert in Japanese social analysis. As the Outreach Coordinator at the Center for Japanese Studies, University of Michigan, he continually works to promote understanding of the people, language and culture of Japan.